Alive Again

Ahmadreza Ahmadi

Illustrated by Nahid Kazemi

tiny owl publishing

First published in Persian by Salis Publisher © 2013, Tehran, Iran
This edition published in 2017 © Tiny Owl Publishing Ltd, London

Written by Ahmadreza Ahmadi
Illustrated by Nahid Kazemi
Translated by Azita Rassi
Graphic designer: Elahe Javanmanrd

ISBN 978-1-910328-24-8

A CIP catalogue record of this book is available from the British Library

Last night the wind blew the blossom from the trees.

"When blossom goes, does the word 'blossom' die?" asked a boy.

"Can there ever be blossom again?"

For a long time no rain fell. The boy asked, "When there is no rain, does the word 'rain' die, so that it can never rain again?"

"If no wheat grows, will the word 'wheat' die, so that wheat can never grow again?" asked the boy.

"If nobody is going on
a journey, does the word
'journey' die so that there can
never be journeys again?"
asked the boy.

When spring came again, the boy's father said,
"Look! New blossom has been born. The word
'blossom' is alive again."

Rain came, raining all night,

so that the word 'rain' was born again.

The rain has fallen on to the wheat grains
in the ground. Now the wheat will grow, and
the word wheat will be born again.

Tomorrow will be the day for
a journey, and then the word
'journey' will be born again.

About the book

This deceptively simple story book is puzzling because it leaves so much unexplained. But it is exactly those gaps in the narrative that leave room for the child's imagination to fill out the story in their own individual ways, making it a perfect starting point for creative work. Ask children to fill those story gaps. Tell me about the boy. Who does he live with? Why is he worried about the blossom going? What journey might he like to go on? The book's collage artwork might inspire similar artwork of their own.

About the author

Ahmadreza Ahmadi is an Iranian poet and children's story writer.
In **2010** he was shortlisted for the 'Hans Christian Andersen' Award.
Ahmadreza Ahmadi's writing style lies somewhere between poetry and
fictional narrative.
Its profound simplicity speaks to both adults and children.